# Lonely
# LULA
# CAT

# *Lonely* LULA CAT

by Joseph Slate
pictures by Bruce Degen

HARPER & ROW, PUBLISHERS

Other books by Joseph Slate

The Star Rocker

How Little Porcupine Played Christmas

The Mean, Clean, Giant Canoe Machine

Library of Congress Cataloging in Publication Data
Slate, Joseph.
  Lonely Lula Cat.
  Summary: While searching for her old friends who now
live far away, lonely Lula Cat discovers new friends
close by.
  1. Children's stories, American.   [1. Cats—Fiction.
2. Friendship—Fiction]   I. Degen, Bruce, ill.
II. Title.
PZ7.S6289Lo  1985      [E]       84-48345
ISBN 0-06-025806-3
ISBN 0-06-025807-1 (lib. bdg.)

            1 2 3 4 5 6 7 8 9 10
                 First Edition

For Luella Griffin and friend Jerry.

—J.S.

For Madeline, who flies to the arms
of loving friends every year.

—B.D.

A slipper moon sailed
by the window.
Lula Cat sat up.
She was in a new bed,
in a new house,
far away from her friends.

"I miss my friends,"
she cried. "I am so lonely."
A tear slid down her nose.
It slipped on a whisker.
It dropped like a bright bead
in moonlight.
Suddenly, a star rocked in
the window.
"I know what I'll do," said
Lula Cat.
"I will wish on Star."

"Star, Star," said Lula Cat,
"I am far away from my friends.
Can you rock me to them?"
Star said, "I can't do that.
They are too far away.
But I can take you to Moon.
Come ride in my saddle,
but no fair spitting."

Lula Cat gave Star a kiss.
Star rocked as they rode.
*Creak—creak. Creak—creak.*
Back and forth, back and forth.
"This is as far as I can go,"
said Star. "Here is Moon."

"Moon, Moon," said Lula Cat,
"I am so lonely. Can you
sail me to my friends?"
"I can't sail that far,"
said Moon. "Maybe Owl can.
I will take you to Owl.
Come ride on my lap,
but don't scratch."

Lula Cat drew in her claws.
She hugged Moon tight.
Moon slapped the clouds
as she sailed.
*Spa-lash! Spa-lash!*
Up and down, up and down.
"This is as far as I can go,"
said Moon. "Here is Owl."

"Owl, Owl," said Lula Cat,
"I miss my friends. Can you
fly me to them?"
"Come sit on my back," said Owl,
"but don't rock. It makes me sick."

Lula Cat sat very still.
Owl's wings fanned Lula Cat's fur.
*Flop—flop. Flop—flop.*

Owl flew in Lula Cat's window. "But this is where I started from," said Lula Cat. "My friends are not here. They are still far away."

"We will see," said Owl.
He spread his wings.
"Pull a feather," said Owl.
"Dip it in ink, and write
a letter to your friends."

Lula Cat wrote a letter.
She said each word as she wrote.

"Dear Friends:
How are you?
I rode on Star, Moon, and Owl.
Owl would not let me rock.
He said, 'It makes me sick.'
I did not rock. I miss you
very much.
Love, Lula Cat."

"Now," said Owl. "I will
fly this letter to your friends.
You are heavy. It is light."
And off Owl flew.

The next night, Owl came back.
He had a letter in his beak.
"This letter is from your friends,"
he said.
"Thank you, Owl," said Lula Cat.
"This is a nice letter.
All the lines go uphill.
Those are the best kind."

"What does it say?"
asked Owl.
Lula Cat read:

"Dear Lula Cat:
We miss you, too. We would
like to ride on Moon, Star,
and Owl. It is fun to do
new things. It is fun to have
new friends. You are lucky,
Lula Cat.
Love, Your Friends."

"That is a nice slanty letter,"
said Owl, leaning sideways.
"Yes," said Lula Cat.
She put the letter in a box.
"But I still wish my old friends
were right here."
"I know," said Owl.
"But you have new friends here.
Guess who."

"Could it be Star?"
guessed Lula Cat.
"Maybe," said Owl.
"Could it be Moon?"
guessed Lula Cat.
"Perhaps," said Owl.

"Could it be…you?" asked Lula Cat.
Owl spun his head like a top.
He made fast side steps.
"Who?" he asked.
"You, Owl.
You flew my letter.
You let me pull a feather.
And you never said, 'Ouch!'"

Owl blinked.
"Yes," he said gruffly.
"We are all your new friends.
We like you, Lula Cat.
You hugged Moon.
You kissed Star.
You never made me sick."

Lula Cat and Owl
sat on the window sill.
"Good night, Star,"
called Lula Cat.
"Good night, Moon,"
called Owl.
Star twinkled. Moon dipped.
Owl and Cat sat very still.